Rocket Rules!

KT-446-701

Written by
Nathan Bryon

Illustrated by
Dapo Adeola

This book belongs to

....

I celebrated World Book Day 2022 with this gift from my local bookseller
and Penguin Random House #ShareAStory

PUFFIN BOOKS is part of the Penguin Random House group
of companies whose addresses can be found at
global.penguinrandomhouse.com.

First published 2022
Text copyright © Nathan Bryon, 2022
Illustrations copyright © Dapo Adeola, 2022
The moral right of the author and illustrator has been asserted

All correspondence to: Puffin Books, Penguin Random House Children's,
One Embassy Gardens, 8 Viaduct Gardens, London SW11 7BW

ISBN: 978-0-241-55888-1
Printed in China   001

WORLD BOOK DAY
World Book Day's mission is to offer every child and young person
the opportunity to read and love books by giving you the chance
to have a book of your own.

To find out more, and for fun activities including our monthly book club,
video stories and book recommendations, visit worldbookday.com.

World Book Day is a charity funded by publishers and booksellers
in the UK and Ireland.

World Book Day is also made possible by generous sponsorship from
National Book Tokens and support from authors and illustrators.

FSC® MIX Paper from responsible sources FSC® C018179

PUFFIN

Hi! I'm Rocket!

My family says one day I'm going to change the world. But every day I like to make a difference - even if it's just something super small.

Follow my **Rocket Rules** and you can make a difference too . . .

Rule 1: Wake Up!

Then jump, dance, fly out of bed!

Ask yourself: What do I want
to learn about the world today?

Today I've decided to learn about insects.

DID YOU KNOW
There are around 5,000
different species
of ladybird!

Make sure you don't miss any
of the wonderful things in the world.

Don't let something **amazing** whizz past you . . .

Rule 3: Read Up!

Even if you find reading hard, take your time –
you can find out all about the world from books . . .

DID YOU KNOW
Reading helps your
brain develop!

Rule 4: Eat Up!

You can't change the world on an empty stomach!

What food do **you** love?

What food will **you** try?

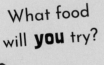

What food will **you** learn to cook?

(Always ask a grown-up for help with cooking!)

Rule 5:
Speak Up!

Don't ever be afraid
to say what you believe.
The world wants to hear you!

SAVE THE
BOOKS

Rule 6: Stand Up

for the things you believe are **GOOD** and **FAIR**.

Rule 7: Clean Up!

Start by tidying your bedroom . . .

. . . and end by tidying the world!

Rule 8: Rise Up!

It's OK to feel sad sometimes . . .

Remember you will **RISE UP** happy again and **READY TO GO!**

Rule 9: Grow Up!

To be whoever or whatever **YOU** want to be!

Rule 10:
Don't Give Up!

Especially on your dreams.
You can make them come true -
you just have to believe!

What's your **biggest** dream?

Some more brilliant books to
Read Up!

LOOK UP!

by Nathan Bryan   illustrated by Dapo Adeola

CLEAN UP!

Nathan Bryan   Dapo Adeola

SPEAK UP!

Coming soon!

HEY YOU!

AN EMPOWERING CELEBRATION OF GROWING UP BLACK

DAPO ADEOLA

MALORIE BLACKMAN   DAPO ADEOLA

WE'RE GOING TO FIND THE MONSTER!